Daisy's Defining Day

Written by Sandra V. Feder

Illustrated by Susan Mitchell

Kids Can Press

To my mentor and first editor, Sheila Barry, who believed in *Daisy* from the start and made all my words better — S.V.F.

For sweet Sadie and happy Holly — S.M.

Contents

Chapter One

Daisy liked knowing all the words to a song and singing them loudly while she danced around the house. She liked making cookies and using at least three different colors of frosting to decorate them. She liked making friendship bracelets with her best friend, Emma, and swearing to Emma that she would never take hers off.

Daisy especially liked riding her bike to the library to check out books. Books were full of words. And even more than making cookies or singing loudly, Daisy loved words. She kept track of her favorite words in a green notebook covered with purple polka dots.

On this particular day, Daisy carried her notebook in her backpack on the way to school. Now that it was early spring, Daisy and Emma often walked with their neighbor, Samantha. They used to try to avoid Samantha because she had only wanted to use words like *stop* and *mine*. But now Samantha was a lot more fun.

The only problem was that walking with Samantha also meant walking with

Samantha's younger brother, Grant. He and his friends used words like *smelly* and *gross*. Usually, the girls didn't pay much attention to Grant, but today, Daisy found herself listening to his conversation.

"We learned about rhymes yesterday," he said. Daisy thought about her list of *Favorite Rhyming Words*. *Sweet* and *treat* were on it, as were *sun* and *fun*. Daisy was just about to share one of her favorite rhymes when Grant shared one of his.

"Sister blister," he said, sticking his tongue out at Samantha.

"That's not very nice," Daisy said. Grant

looked at Daisy, and then a not-so-nice smile spread across his face. "Lazy Daisy," he said.

"Don't listen to him," Samantha advised. "I never do."

Daisy tried, but soon Grant and all his friends were chanting, "Lazy Daisy!" Luckily, they were distracted by a trail of ants crossing the sidewalk. "Grant the Ant," Daisy thought to herself, but swallowed the words before they came out. By the time they got to the school playground, Grant seemed to have forgotten about his new nickname for Daisy. But just before he headed to his classroom, he yelled, "Bye, Lazy Daisy!" in such a loud voice that many of the older kids turned and looked at her. Samantha mouthed, "Sorry," to Daisy as they walked into Room 8.

Daisy put her green notebook with the purple polka dots away in her desk and sat down. But she kept thinking about Grant's chant.

What if everyone in the whole school started calling her Lazy Daisy?

There was only one word that could describe how she would feel then — *miserable*.

Chapter Two

Daisy didn't have too much time to worry, because it was a demanding day for the students in Room 8. They had to write a story using all their spelling words from the last week, and then they had a math test on fractions. After the test, fractions were filling Daisy's head so completely that she couldn't think a whole thought. And Daisy wasn't alone. All the students looked as though their heads were a little too full.

So Miss Goldner, the best teacher in the world, put her hands on her hips and said, "You know what we need right now? A dance break! But this time, we're going to add a twist." Daisy and Emma wondered what kind of a twist. Would she teach them a pretzel dance? Would she make them hold hands, get all tangled up, and then try to untangle themselves without letting go of each other's hands? But Miss Goldner didn't say anything more. She just walked to the CD player and pushed a button. When "The Twist" came on, Miss Goldner demonstrated for the class. Pretty soon, everyone in Room 8 was giggling and twisting to the beat.

After the dance break, Miss Goldner gave each student a blank piece of paper.

"We're going to have some fun writing sentences about animals. But the *twist* here is going to be that all the words in the sentence have to start with the same letter or sound as the animal's name," Miss Goldner said. "That's called alliteration. Let's have fun with all the letters, starting with *A*. For instance, you might write 'Angry Alligators Ate Apples' or 'Bossy Beavers Bit Bark.'"

Daisy thought the animal sentences were fabulous! She started with "Awesome Antelopes Are Athletic" and was all the way to "Handy Hippos Hammer Houses" when the bell rang signaling the end of the day.

Emma and Daisy talked about the assignment all the way home. "I love how the words sound together," Daisy said, sharing her favorite sentence of the day. "Elegant Elephants Eagerly Eat Éclairs." Daisy couldn't wait to enter the animal sentences into her notebook.

Chapter Three

But when Daisy turned to go up her driveway, Grant was standing there. Although she now liked having Samantha living next door, Daisy wished Grant could live somewhere else.

"Look! It's Lazy Daisy," Grant said.

Daisy tried her hardest to ignore him as Samantha had suggested. Daisy remembered that she had used the same technique last week when Will, who sat next to her at school, took her favorite lavender mechanical pencil and twirled it around in his hand. Daisy simply ignored him and took out a new pencil. After recess, she noticed that her pencil had been returned unharmed.

But something about Lazy Daisy really bothered her. Maybe it was because she had always thought her name was quite wonderful. It was fun to say, not too long or too short, unique and, of course, flowery.

So after thinking for a minute, she took off her backpack, went into the side yard and dragged out a large garbage can.

"What are you doing?" Grant asked.

"My chore," Daisy answered.

"But no one told you to do it right now," Grant said.

"I know," Daisy responded, "but I want to get it done. I don't want to be *lazy* and put it off until later." She hoped he would get the message.

Grant nodded. Daisy felt a bit of relief as she pulled the garbage can to the curb. Grant played basketball while Daisy went back into the side yard and carried out a large container filled with paper and cardboard to be recycled. Even though she wanted a snack, she wanted to make her point even more. So she decided she wouldn't stop until Grant had gone inside. Back into the side yard she went to bring out the plastic recyclables and the compost bin. Finally, Grant hugged his ball to his chest. Then he turned and called out, "Bye, Lazy Daisy," as if it were so clearly her name that he didn't even have to think twice before saying it.

"Arrgh!" Daisy groaned, before she stomped inside.

To make herself feel better, Daisy turned to her favorite things — words. She thought about alliteration and tried to come up with words that not only started with the same letter or sound but also fit well together. Soon she had a list called *Perfectly Paired Words*. *Bouncy balls* and *chunky chocolate* were on the list along with *flying flags* and *summer sun*.

Daisy was so pleased with her list she decided to share it with Mrs. Bookman, her neighbor.

"Happy hello, nice neighbor," Daisy said, waving her hand, when Mrs. Bookman opened the door.

"Hello, Daisy," Mrs. Bookman said. "Would you like a snack?"

Daisy was always happy when Mrs. Bookman offered her a snack. Mrs. Bookman often had unusual foods to eat. Today, she passed Daisy a bowl full of edamame, which she said were soybeans.

Daisy opened one and munched it.

"Crispy and crunchy!" she declared.

Mrs. Bookman smiled. "I can't help
but notice you are using alliteration today,"
she said.

"Yes, I am," Daisy said. "We learned about
it at school."

Then Daisy thought for a minute.

"It's fabulously fun!" she said.

Mrs. Bookman thought, too.

"And mighty memorable!" she responded.

Daisy gave Mrs. Bookman a high five and then explained the exercise Miss Goldner had done with them. Mrs. Bookman listened carefully, offering Daisy some grapefruit soda to wash down her edamame. Then Daisy shared her list of *Perfectly Paired Words*.

"Lovely list!" Mrs. Bookman exclaimed.

Daisy headed home with her mind full of wonderful word combinations and her tummy full of super snacks. She was in such a good mood that she didn't even mind when her mother asked her to finish her homework before dinner. After dinner, it took three long games of dominoes with her father before she finally won. To celebrate her victory, she did a happy dance.

But later that night, after she was in bed, her mind drifted back to Grant. She hoped he wouldn't remember Lazy Daisy the next day. She distracted herself by thinking about chewy chunky chocolate chip cookies until she fell asleep. But in her dream that night, her chocolate chip cookie crumbs attracted ants, and she couldn't figure out how to get rid of them.

Chapter Four

When Daisy woke up, she couldn't shake the uneasy feeling she had from her dream.

"That's silly," she told herself. "It was just a dream." But as she stepped onto the playground at school, Grant called out, "Hi, Lazy Daisy." Then he did it again twice during recess. By the time school ended, Daisy needed a break.

"You go ahead without me," she told her friends. "I want to help Miss Goldner."

"I'll help, too," Emma said. Daisy smiled. Emma always seemed to know when Daisy needed her. Daisy and Emma stapled handouts for the next day.

"I'll be sad when Miss Goldner gets married and moves away," Daisy said.

"Me, too," answered Emma. "But at least we have her until the end of the school year."

Daisy nodded.

The girls said good-bye to Miss Goldner and headed home.

"Bye, Daisy," Emma said — without any *lazy*, of course — as Daisy turned to go up her driveway.

***

Daisy plopped down on the stool at the kitchen counter and told her mom all about her day. As excited as Daisy was about the new animal sentences she had added to her notebook that day, she couldn't help hearing Grant's chant of "Lazy Daisy." She even remembered how a few of his friends had kept it up on the playground at lunchtime.

"I wish I had a name that would stick better than Lazy Daisy," she said.

"Well, I still like to call you Daisy Bug," her mom said.

"Thanks, but that's not quite what I was

looking for," Daisy said. "I need a name that's so great it will make everyone forget Lazy Daisy."

"Everyone's so busy all the time," her mother said. "I think being lazy is nice once in a while."

Despite her mother's words, Daisy didn't see how being called lazy could be anything but awful. A spectacular new name was definitely what she needed. Daisy thought about rhymes. Maybe she could come up with one that would make everyone forget *lazy*. But Crazy Daisy was even worse than Lazy Daisy, and Hazy Daisy wasn't any better. She went into the backyard and tried to skip rope 50 times in a row. She got to 37 before her foot caught and she barely stopped herself from falling.

Daisy lay down in the hammock to read over some of her favorite word lists from her notebook. She had recently made a new one called *Cloud Words*. She had *cotton candy*, *white*, *gray* and *floating*. Today, Daisy looked up and added the word *wispy*. She had just learned that *wispy* meant fine or feathery and thought it perfectly described the clouds above her.

Because she was still restless, even after some quiet

cloud watching, Daisy decided to go inside
to talk to Bubbles, her pet fish, who came
when she called his name. Talking to Bubbles
and looking at the clear water usually helped
clear her head, which was feeling particularly
cloudy today. But even Bubbles didn't help.

She played with the friendship bracelet on her wrist that Emma had made for her last week. Emma had used threads that were yellow, purple and turquoise, which were all of Daisy's favorite colors. The one Daisy had made for Emma was three different shades of pink. Just the way Emma liked it.

Finally, Daisy sat down and turned to her newest list, *Perfectly Paired Words*, and read some of the word pairs to herself. "That's it!" she said out loud. She quickly closed the notebook and called out to her mom, "I'm going to Emma's," as she headed out the door.

Chapter Five

Daisy raced on her bike to Emma's house. "I'm going to come up with a name that is so great everyone will forget Lazy Daisy," she told Emma, who was practicing ballet pirouettes in the front yard.

"Dynamite!" Emma said.

"That's great," Daisy said. "I love it!"

Emma looked confused.

"*Dynamite* Daisy," Daisy explained. "I'm going to use alliteration, like we did in class, to come up with the perfect name. We should come up with one for you, too."

Emma's pirouette kicked up a cloud of dirt. "*Dusty* Daisy?" Daisy wondered as she brushed herself off. She shook her head.

"I'm feeling a little dizzy," Emma said, after her fourth pirouette in a row.

"*Dizzy* Daisy?" Daisy asked. No. She knew she could do better.

"We need to find some really good words," Daisy said. "Let's try the library."

"*Mahatzi!*" Emma replied, using Daisy's made-up word for "let's go!"

The girls got on their bikes and rode to the nearby branch of the public library. They each took a book off the shelf and started looking.

"What about *drowsy?*" Emma asked.

"I think that means sleepy," Daisy answered.

"How about *expensive* for you?" Daisy asked. "It starts with an *E.*"

"My dad says it costs a lot of money for my dance lessons," Emma said. "But I don't think I want that in my name."

"How about *dreamy?*" Emma suggested, looking at a different book with a sleeping bear on its cover.

"*Drowsy* and *dreamy,*" Daisy said, yawning. "You're putting me to sleep! I think we need to get out of here."

The girls decided to head downtown on

their bikes to see if a little exercise would wake them up. As they passed Sweetums, the best candy store in the world, Daisy got a good idea. "*Delicious*," she said out loud.

Emma thought for a minute. "My mother calls my baby cousin *delicious*, especially after she's just had her bath. But I'm not sure it's right for a bigger kid."

After a few more blocks, the girls locked up their bikes and set out on foot. The jewelry store was advertising *diamond* earrings. Daisy had been born in April, which made the diamond her birthstone. The girls pressed their faces against the store window to get a better look. The diamonds were pretty and sparkly but not quite right to be a part of Daisy's name.

At a clothing store displaying "Elegant Dresses for Special Occasions," the girls stopped and looked at the pretty gowns. "You could be *Elegant* Emma," Daisy said, sashaying across the sidewalk. "Nah," said Emma. "I don't feel old enough for elegant."

The girls walked and talked some more. Soon, they were in front of the movie theater. They stopped and stared. It was amazing!

All the movie posters were full of wonderful words! *Divine* and *dazzling* were used to describe one coming attraction about a girl who suddenly becomes a pop sensation. The main characters of an adventure, a young girl and her talking puppy, were called *delightful* and *dependable*.

On the opposite wall, the beautiful star of a romantic comedy was *entertaining* and *enchanting*, while a drama set in outer space was *extraordinary* and *exciting*. Daisy quickly took out her notebook and wrote down each of their favorites: *extraordinary* and *enchanting* for Emma and *dazzling* and *delightful* for Daisy.

Chapter Six

The girls decided to skip Sweetums and instead headed for the frozen yogurt store, which had recently opened. It was the type of place where you could pick your flavor of yogurt and then add toppings. Emma chose blueberry yogurt with fresh strawberries and peaches on top. Daisy chose chocolate yogurt with cookie pieces.

Daisy thought about bringing home some frozen yogurt for her younger sister, Lily, because she liked surprising Lily with little gifts, but decided against it. The frozen yogurt would just be a cup of melted yogurt soup by the time Daisy got it home. The girls sat down at a table to eat and chat.

"We found some really good words for our names," Daisy said.

"But how do we put them all together?" Emma asked.

"I'm not quite sure yet," Daisy said. "Anyway, I think we still need a few more."

"More?" asked Emma. "Are you sure?"

"Yep," said Daisy. "I want a really great name that everyone will remember."

"Sounds good to me," Emma said, as they finished up their yogurt and prepared to head home.

* * *

That night at the dinner table, Daisy told her family about her day looking for words.

"We found some at the library, but they weren't quite right," she explained. "But the movie theater posters were full of wonderful words. Maybe I should be an actress." Daisy considered this for a moment. Then, all of a sudden, she gasped loudly and let her head drop to the table, being careful to just miss the plate of food in front of her. She kept one eye open to see her family's reaction. The only one who looked a little alarmed was Lily, who asked, "Daisy okay?" Her mother just smiled and said, "Very dramatic, my dear." Daisy lifted up her head and nodded. Hmmm. *Dramatic* might be a useful word to have in her name. If she were *Dramatic Daisy*, she could act out whenever she pleased.

After dinner, Daisy played checkers with Lily. But when Daisy got into bed, her head was so full of words beginning with the letter D that she didn't think she'd ever be able to fall asleep. She sat up, reached over to her nightstand and picked up her green notebook with the purple polka dots. She opened it to her list of *Quiet-Time Words* and smiled as she read

good-night, snuggle, hush-a-bye, lullaby and *sweet dreams.* She added *dreamy* and *drowsy.*

Daisy smiled again. She loved it when she thought a list was finished and then, when she wasn't even thinking about that list at all, she came across new words to make it even better!

Daisy lay down and, instead of counting sheep, recited all the words beginning with the letter *D* that she had come across that day. As she said each one, she pictured the words jumping over a fence and dancing away. By the time she got to the word *dreamy,* she started to feel a little *drowsy* and soon fell asleep.

Chapter Seven

The next day was science day, so Daisy
and Emma got to school earlier than usual.
Miss Goldner always made science fun. But
when they got there and put their backpacks
away, they couldn't believe the mess they saw.
There were strips of newspaper on every desk
and table, big pieces of cardboard against the
walls and bottles of all different sizes on the
carpet at the front of the room.

"What happened in here?" Will asked

when he came in. Daisy and Emma were wondering the same thing.

"Oh, nothing," Miss Goldner said, coming into the classroom with her arms full of bottles of starch and a bright red apron on over her clothes. "It's papier-mâché day!"

"I want to make an elephant!" Samantha announced.

"Well, that would be fun," Miss Goldner answered, "but today, we're going to make land forms. We're turning these bottles into mountains. But first, we're going to talk about them. And let's have some fun!" Then a little smile crept onto her face. "Perhaps they'll be *mighty* mountains," she said.

"Or *mammoth* mountains," Ben called out, picking up on Miss Goldner's use of *M* words.

"Or *majestic* mountains," Daisy offered.

"Exactly!" Miss Goldner said. "And let's not forget our oceans."

"*Open* oceans," Emma offered.

"How about grasslands?" Miss Goldner asked. By now, the students really had the hang of it. They called out *green* and *graceful,* and for bays, the students added *blue* and *bright.*

"Now that we have described our land forms so well, let's get to work," Miss Goldner said, handing out smocks to the class. One group made *beautiful bright blue bays,* one made *majestic* and *mighty mountains* and one made *graceful green grasslands.* And absolutely everyone got covered with starch and had a marvelous time.

* * *

Daisy and Samantha had made plans to finish their handball battle at recess. So far, they had each won two games. The girls raced outside to make sure they got their favorite handball wall, and Emma stood off to the side to be scorekeeper. It was a fierce battle, and Daisy put up a good fight. The score was tied before the final serve. But Samantha triumphed by hitting the ball just outside Daisy's range. Daisy was exhausted, but she still gave Samantha a high five as they sat on a bench to catch their breath. Just then, Grant walked by and called, in a not unfriendly way, "Hi, Sammy and Lazy Daisy!"

Daisy couldn't believe it! Lazy? Hadn't she just played her hardest! She'd like to see *him* almost beat Samantha.

Daisy decided she had better choose her new name as soon as possible.

Chapter Eight

At home that afternoon, Daisy got right to work. When her mother offered her an after-school snack, Daisy just shook her head.

"You seem very determined today," her mother said.

"I've got to decide on my new name," Daisy said. "And it has to be just right."

Daisy looked at the list she had compiled:

Dynamite from Emma.

Dazzling and *delightful* from the movie posters.

Dusty and *dizzy* had been crossed out.

Dreamy and *drowsy* had question marks next to them.

Delicious had a picture of a slice of pizza next to it.

Dramatic had a star next to it.

Lastly, she added *determined*.

She wrote down many combinations and practiced saying them out loud.

"*Dreamy Dynamite Delicious Daisy*," she tried. No, not quite right.

Finally, after many more tries, Daisy felt certain she had it.

She put on her favorite red feather boa and ran to find her mother and Lily.

"Drum roll, please," Daisy said to Lily,

who obliged by playing air drums and saying, "Da-da-da-daaa!"

"Presenting me, *Dynamite Dramatic Determined Dazzling Daisy!*"

"Wow!" said her mother. "I certainly am dazzled."

"Me, too!" said Lily, although she wasn't quite sure what dazzled meant.

"I've got to go tell Emma," Daisy said, taking her boa with her as she ran out the door.

"Bye, *Dynamic Dazzle Daisy*," Lily called.

Daisy frowned for just a moment. "That's okay," she said to Lily. "I'll teach you the right way to say it when I get home."

Chapter Nine

"Dynamite Dramatic Determined Dazzling Daisy!" she said, twirling around Emma's front yard.

"Coolio!" Emma said, using the word she and Daisy had made up. They used it when something was so super that no other word would quite do. It was such a good word, they had wondered if someone else might have discovered it first.

"I think I'll be Exciting Extraordinary

Emma," Emma said.

Daisy stopped twirling for a minute. "It's a little short," she said.

Emma just smiled and said, "I like it!"

Daisy, who was *determined,* appreciated that same quality in her best friend. "Then *Exciting Extraordinary Emma* it is!"

The girls decided to go inside and practice writing their new names with Emma's sparkly gel pens.

Emma, whose name was a bit shorter, wrote hers five times using five different colors. Because it took Daisy a little longer, she was only able to write hers three times,

with three different colors, before it was time
to go home. But she didn't mind. She loved
her new name and was sure everyone else
would, too.

* * *

When she got home, she played Go Fish with
Lily before dinner.

"Daisy! Lily! Please come set the table,"
their mother called.

Daisy was shocked.

"Please use my full name," Daisy
responded, in her most adult-sounding voice.

"Daisy Ann," her mother said. "Please
come to the kitchen."

"Not that full name," Daisy said. "My new name!"

So Daisy's mother tried again. "*Dazzling Dynamite Daisy? Dramatic Determined Daisy? Determined Dynamite Dramatic Daisy?*"

But even with three more tries, she couldn't get it right. Lily set the table and picked which bowl of macaroni and cheese she wanted. Daisy just knew Lily had picked the cheesiest. Finally, Daisy's mother remembered the new and amazing name. *"Dynamite Dramatic Determined Dazzling Daisy!"* she called, and Daisy came running. She was starved.

At dinner, between bites, she tried to teach her new name to her dad and Lily.

"Dynamite is something that blows things up, but it also means 'great' and it's the first thing Emma said when I told her about coming up with a new name. *Dramatic* is

because I'm an actress," she said, letting out a very dramatic sigh and laying the back of her hand across her forehead.

"Very dramatic," her father agreed.

"*Determined* is because that's what Mom says I am a lot of the time. And *dazzling* is because it sounds fabulous."

"Well, it certainly is a fabulous name," her mother said.

"Definitely!" said her father.

"*Dramatical Dazzle Daisy!*" Lily said, happily.

"No," Daisy said firmly. "It's *Dynamite Dramatic Determined Dazzling Daisy.*"

"Can you write it down for me on a little piece of paper I can keep in my wallet?" her father asked. "That way, I can look at it and it will be easier for me to learn."

"Sure," Daisy said, going over to a drawer in the kitchen to take out a piece of paper, a pen and some scissors.

"Time for dessert," her mother said, putting out a plate of homemade sugar cookies.

"*Delicious*," everyone agreed.

Chapter Ten

The next morning, Daisy's mother called out, "Time to get up, *Dynamite Dramatic Determined Dazzling Daisy!*"

Daisy was so pleased with her new name and the fact that her mother had gotten it right that she leapt out of bed.

On the way to school, Daisy and Emma taught Samantha their new names. By the time they got to the edge of the playground at school, Samantha had both names down.

Emma remembered to use Daisy's long name for most of the morning. But by lunchtime, she was a little worn out.

"Do you think I can just call you *Dazzling Daisy?*" she asked. Daisy couldn't believe it! After all the time she had spent working on her name, her best friend wasn't even willing to use it. Samantha had given up at recess, calling out, "Handball rematch, Daisy?" Daisy had refused to answer.

But she simply couldn't refuse to answer Emma. Not Emma. So she sighed, "No, please use my full name."

And Emma, because she was Daisy's best friend, did.

"*Dynamite Dramatic Determined Dazzling Daisy*, what are you doing after school today?" Emma asked.

"Well, *Exciting Extraordinary Emma*, I'm going to help Lily learn to ride the new bike she got for her birthday."

The rest of the school day, Daisy thought Emma seemed a little less chatty than usual. But maybe it was just her imagination.

* * *

On the way home, Grant walked with the girls. Just as he opened his mouth to say, "Hi, Lazy Daisy," Daisy held up her hand.

"My name is *Dynamite Dramatic Determined Dazzling Daisy*," she said, quite dramatically.

Grant didn't know what to say. So he said nothing at all. Daisy breathed a sigh of relief.

As Emma turned to head home, she started to say, "Bye, Dais …" but stopped. Instead she just said, "Bye," and hurried off.

Daisy called after her, "Bye, *Exciting Extraordinary Emma!*"

Emma turned and waved but didn't say anything.

Chapter Eleven

After having a snack, Daisy helped Lily put on her helmet. But before Lily would even consider getting onto her new bike, she spent a good ten minutes finding things to put into the white basket that was attached to the front. First, Lily put in a water bottle, which Daisy had to admit was practical. But when Lily added a sweatshirt, a granola bar and a single mitten that had been lying in the garage, Daisy thought it was enough. "We're not going very far," she said. "We're just going to practice in front of the house for a while."

"Just one more thing," Lily said. "I need my lucky scarf." Lily ran back into the house and emerged a few minutes later with an orange bandanna tied around her neck. Their mother had gotten it for her to wear to Western Day at school last month. Lily had loved learning to square dance, and when her foursome won an award for best dancing, she had decided the scarf was "lucky."

Finally, Lily was ready to go. Daisy taught Lily how to walk the bike down the driveway, carefully holding onto the handlebars. When they were on the sidewalk, she helped Lily get on the bike. Even though the bike still had training wheels, it wasn't altogether steady on the uneven sidewalk. But Lily quickly got the hang of it, happily riding along with Daisy jogging next to her. When it came time to turn around, Lily yanked the handlebars sharply to the right. Daisy managed to grab the bike before it fell.

"Don't turn so fast," Daisy instructed.

"I'll do it better next time, *Dyna Dazzle Daisy!*" Lily promised. Lily still needed some help getting Daisy's new name right, but Daisy didn't have any time to think more about it because Lily had zoomed ahead.

"Slow down!" Daisy called to her. "And stop at our driveway."

When Daisy and Lily were finished with the lesson, they saw a bunch of kids gathering for a neighborhood game of soccer. After making sure Lily and her bike got safely back into the garage, Daisy went to join in.

"Daisy," Samantha called out when it was her turn to pick someone for her team. Daisy started to walk over to Samantha but stopped.

"Please use my full name," she said.

Samantha nodded.

"*Drama Dazzling Daisy,*" she tried.

"Determinable Dramatical Daisy?" she asked.
But Samantha couldn't get it right. The
other kids wanted to get started, so Samantha
picked someone else. Daisy sat and watched.
The only good part was that Grant didn't say
anything to her.

When Daisy got home, she decided to help
Lily practice saying her new name.

"Dynamite Dramatic Dazzle Daisy," was
the best Lily could do. Even though Daisy
was determined to have Lily include the word
determined, Lily seemed just as determined to
leave it out.

Chapter Twelve

When her father got home from work, he found Daisy sitting beneath her favorite tree.

"How's *Dynamite Dramatic Determined Dazzling Daisy?*" he asked.

"Feeling like *discouraged* Daisy," she answered.

Her father sat down next to her on the grass, even though he was still wearing his work clothes.

"Why is that?" he asked.

"Because even though I have a fabulous new name, no one wants to use it," she said. "I missed out on the cheesiest bowl of macaroni and cheese last night, handball at recess and soccer after school."

Lily rode by on her bicycle and waved. She had been riding around while Daisy was outside on the lawn.

"Hmm," said her father. "Well, I do think your name is fabulous."

"I guess so," Daisy said. "But maybe it's just too hard to use."

"Definitely a difficult dilemma, Daisy," her father said.

"Good alliteration!" Daisy remarked as her dad headed inside.

After a few minutes, Daisy's mother called out, "Dinner!" Lily, who was zooming along, turned her head. Then, without putting on the brake, Lily yanked the handlebars sharply to turn around. The bike toppled over and Lily let out a cry.

"Daisy!" she yelled.

And then a funny thing happened. Daisy didn't think, even for a second, about the fact that Lily hadn't used her full name. She didn't think about all the time she had spent teaching it to Lily that very afternoon. All she thought about was getting to her sister.

"I'm coming, Lily!" she yelled, running down the driveway.

Daisy rolled up Lily's pants to check her knees for scrapes and then checked the palms of her hands. Daisy brushed off the dirt and

took off Lily's helmet. Then Daisy gently held Lily's hand, so as not to rub the part that was scraped, as they walked back to the house.

"You need a little first aid," Daisy said when they got inside. Daisy sat Lily down on the couch and wiped away her tears. Then Daisy disappeared for a minute and came back wearing a nurse's hat and holding a bunch of brightly colored Band-Aids, a bottle of antiseptic spray and a box of tissues.

"Nurse Daisy at your service!" Daisy announced. First Daisy cleaned the scrapes with the spray and some tissues.

"Does this need a Band-Aid?" Daisy asked, pointing to the scrape on Lily's right knee. Lily nodded.

"How about the other knee?" Daisy asked.

"That one, too," Lily answered.

Lily wanted Band-Aids on her hands as well.

"Does it hurt here, too?" Daisy asked as she pointed to Lily's arm, which hadn't gotten scraped at all.

"Oh, yes," Lily replied.

"And here?" Daisy asked, pointing to her nose. Lily giggled as she nodded again.

Soon both girls were giggling happily as Daisy put on more Band-Aids. When they

were all done, Lily raced to show her mother.

"Oh, my," said her mother. "Did you take a bad fall or just have a very nice nurse?"

Lily looked over at Nurse Daisy and said, "Thank you, *Dynamite Dramatic Dazzle Daisy!*"

***

That night, Daisy was totally *kersapped*, her made-up word for the confusion she was feeling. She loved her fabulous new name, but she did have to admit that it was a bit long to use in everyday conversation. And her new name had meant missing out on things she enjoyed.

Then she thought about Grant. She disliked being called Lazy Daisy so much that she thought about sticking with her new name. But there was something even worse than missing out on things she enjoyed and even worse than being called

Lazy Daisy. She really didn't like that her name was hard for her best friend to use.

Daisy got up, took out her notebook and started a new list called *Friendship Words*. She wrote down *fun*, *laugh* and *share*. Then she looked at the friendship bracelet on her wrist. It was a bit tattered, and the bright colors had faded since the day Emma had tied it on Daisy's arm. They had promised never to take them off, and both girls had kept their word. Daisy added the word *special* to her list. Daisy had made up her mind.

Chapter Thirteen

The next morning, Daisy got up a little
earlier than usual. She risked going through
Mrs. Bookman's bushes, which could
be a little prickly, to get to Emma's
house without going by
Samantha's house.
Today, she needed
to talk to
Emma
alone.

She waited patiently until Emma came out.

"Hi, Emma," she said, waving.

"Hi, Dais ..." Emma stopped. "I mean *Dynamite Dramatic Determined Dazzling Daisy.*"

"Thanks," Daisy said, appreciating the effort Emma had made, "but I'm going back to using my regular name."

"Really?" Emma asked.

"I wanted a new, special name to make everyone forget Lazy Daisy," Daisy said. "But my new name was so special no one could remember it. And even if they did remember it, they got tired of saying it all the time."

"Well," Emma said, "I'll still use it if you want."

Daisy looked at the friendship bracelet on her wrist.

"Thanks," she said. "I know you would, but it seemed like you were talking to me less when you had to use my long name. I didn't like that."

"I didn't either," Emma replied.

Then Emma handed Daisy a piece of bright yellow construction paper, which Emma had hidden behind her back. On it she had written in violet-colored glitter glue Daisy's fabulous long name.

"I made this for you," she said handing it

to Daisy. "I figured even if I couldn't say it all the time, you'd still know that I thought it was a really great name."

"I love it!" Daisy said. "And I know just what I'm going to do with it."

DYNAMITE
DRAMATIC
DETERMINED
DAZZLING
DAISY!

Chapter Fourteen

That afternoon, Daisy decided to finish her homework after dinner. She carefully hung the sign Emma had made for her on the door of her bedroom. Then she went outside, lay down on the grass and looked at the sky. She added *fluffy* and *puffy* to her list of *Cloud Words*. She felt the breeze on her face.

Then she counted how many seconds it took each cloud to drift out of her line of sight. "One, two, three, four, five, six, seven,

eight, nine," she said, as a big, white, fluffy
one went by.

Suddenly a shadow appeared. Daisy looked
up to see Grant standing over her, staring.

"What are you doing?" he asked.

"I'm watching the clouds," she said.

"Why?" he asked.

"Because it's nice and peaceful," Daisy
answered.

Then she smiled.

"I'm being lazy," she said, stretching her
arms up over her head.

Grant thought for a minute.

Then he did something surprising.

He lay down next to Daisy and watched the
clouds, too.

"I like this," he said. "It's *different.*"

"I think it's *delightful,*" Daisy said.

They watched a few more clouds go by.

"I guess I like being a little different and a
little lazy," Daisy said.

"Me, too," Grant said. "Too bad *lazy*
doesn't rhyme with my name."

Daisy sat up and laughed — a full out, deep, belly laugh. All this time she hadn't wanted to be Lazy Daisy and now Grant wished he could be lazy just like her!

"I'd like to be lazy some more, but I have to go to basketball practice," Grant said. He got up and walked toward his house. Then he looked over his shoulder at Daisy and waved.

As she lay down again, Daisy thought about her conversation with Grant. And she kept coming back to two words — *delightful* and *different*. That's all she wanted to be.

Delightfully Different Daisy. Just right.

Daisy's Wonderful Word Lists

FAVORITE RHYMING WORDS

sweet — treat

flower — power

sun — fun

bright — light

look — book

ANIMAL ALLITERATIONS

Awesome Antelopes Are Athletic

Big Bears Behave Badly

Clever Cats Claw Couches

Daring Dolphins Dive Deep

Elegant Elephants Eagerly Eat Éclairs

Fluffy Fun Flamingoes Flutter

Glittering Golden Goldfish Glide

Handy Hippos Hammer Houses

PERFECTLY PAIRED WORDS

bouncy balls

chunky chocolate

comfy couches

flying flags

summer sun

CLOUD WORDS

cotton candy   wispy

white   fluffy

gray   puffy

floating

D WORDS

dynamite	delicious	dependable
dusty	diamond	dramatic
dizzy	divine	determined
drowsy	dazzling	different
dreamy	delightful	

E WORDS

expensive	entertaining	extraordinary
elegant	enchanting	exciting

QUIET-TIME WORDS

good-night   sweet dreams

snuggle   dreamy

hush-a-bye   drowsy

lullaby

MADE-UP WORDS

coolio — super

Iska-biska — How are you?

Ilpa-dilpa — Fine, thank you.

Mahatzi — Let's go!

glubby — feeling blah

kersapped — confused

FRIENDSHIP WORDS

fun

laugh

share

special

trust

together

Text © 2013 Sandra V. Feder
Illustrations © 2013 Susan Mitchell

This is a work of fiction and any resemblance of characters to persons living or
dead is purely coincidental.

Kids Can Press acknowledges the financial support of the Government of Ontario,
through the Ontario Media Development Corporation's Ontario Book Initiative;
the Ontario Arts Council; the Canada Council for the Arts; and the Government
of Canada, through the CBF, for our publishing activity.

Many of the designations used by manufacturers and sellers to distinguish their
products are claimed as trademarks. Where those designations appear in this book
and Kids Can Press Ltd. was aware of a trademark claim, the designations have
been printed in initial capital letters (e.g., Band-Aid).

Published in Canada by	Published in the U.S. by
Kids Can Press Ltd.	Kids Can Press Ltd.
25 Dockside Drive	2250 Military Road
Toronto, ON M5A 0B5	Tonawanda, NY 14150

www.kidscanpress.com

Edited by Sheila Barry and Debbie Rogosin
Designed by Marie Bartholomew

CM 13 0 9 8 7 6 5 4 3 2 1

This book is smyth sewn casebound.

Manufactured in Shen Zhen, Guang Dong, P.R. China, in 9/2012
by Printplus Limited

Library and Archives Canada Cataloguing in Publication

Feder, Sandra V., 1963–
    Daisy's defining day / written by Sandra V. Feder ; illustrated by
Susan Mitchell.

(Daisy)
ISBN 978-1-55453-780-8

I. Mitchell, Susan, 1962– II. Title III. Series: Feder, Sandra V., 1963– Daisy.

PZ7.F334Dad 2013   j813'.6   C2012-904397-4

Kids Can Press is a *l*©**ⁿ**ᴜ**s**™ Entertainment company